The Treasure Hunt

First published by Collins in 1951.
Published in Great Britain, 1997, by
Pookie Productions Ltd
12 Craighouse Avenue
Edinburgh EH10 5LN

© Ivy Wallace 1951, 1997

The moral right of the author has been asserted.

British Library Cataloguing-in-Publication Data
A Catalogue record of this book is available
from the British Library.

ISBN 1 872885 54 3

Designed and typeset in 16/20pt Stone Informal
by Mitchell Graphics

Printed and bound in Great Britain
by Cromwell Press, Melksham, Wiltshire

The
Animal Shelf

THE TREASURE HUNT

Written and Illustrated by
Ivy Wallace

POOKIE PRODUCTIONS
Beautiful Books for Children

They all sat on the rug, listening to every word.

THE TREASURE HUNT

One night, Timothy was reading a bedtime story to his Special Animals. They all sat on the rug, listening to every word.

" . . . and so the secret treasure was found at last," read Timothy. "That's the end of the story. It's bedtime now!"

Gumpa the bear and Woeful the monkey, Stripey the zebra, Getup the giraffe and Little Mut climbed up on to their Shelf.

Long after Timothy was asleep, the Animals whispered in the dark.

"I'd like to find treasure," whispered Stripey.

"In the story, they found a mysterious plan first," said Woeful. "They dug where it said 'X' and found treasure. I wish we could find a mysterious plan."

Suddenly Gumpa said, "I found a mysterious plan today!"

"How wonderful!" squealed the others.

"Sssh, we'll wake Timothy," warned Gumpa. "Follow me!" They climbed down from the Shelf, tiptoed out after him and sat in the moonlight on the landing window seat.

Gumpa showed them the mysterious plan.

"I found it in the garden," explained Gumpa proudly.

"It says GOLD!" gasped Getup.

"That 'X' marks the place to dig," said Stripey helpfully.

"I know that, stupid!" said Gumpa. "Tomorrow I'll dig for gold. Let's go back to sleep now!"

Very early, Gumpa woke up and thought of his plan.

"I'll go and dig up my treasure," he decided. "The others will be surprised when they wake and I show it to them!"

The little bear trotted happily through the sleeping house and out into the garden. He took a trowel and the plan.

"Here must be the place marked X!" muttered Gumpa. "Ah, someone's been digging! Burying the treasure, I expect."

He started digging and soon had a deep hole. "What's this? Oh, just a silly old onion!" He threw it to one side. "I must dig deeper still. Oh, here are more onions!"

Suddenly Mr Carr the gardener came rushing up.

*"**B**ear!"* he roared. *"**What are you doing?**"*

"Digging for treasure," replied Gumpa politely, "but I can only find onions."

"Onions!" thundered Mr Carr. *"**Those aren't onions!** They're my valuable lily bulbs! Golden Beauties! And that's my plan, you interfering bear!"*

He hung Gumpa up by his coat and left him dangling.

Back on the Shelf, the others had woken up.

"Gumpa's taken the plan," wailed Woeful. "I've forgotten what was on it."

"Let's each look for treasure!" suggested Getup.

"We'll meet later and show our treasures," agreed Stripey.

The Animals hurried down into the garden.

"I know where I'm going to search!" boasted Woeful. "No-one must watch where I go."

"I'm off too," squeaked Little Mut.

"Let's search together, Stripey," said Getup.

Little Mut met a squirrel. "I'm searching for treasure," he squeaked. "Have you seen any?"

"Plenty, follow me!" said squirrel, darting up a tree.

It took Little Mut half the morning to climb up to see the treasure. "Why, it's just nuts!" he wailed. "I'm looking for gold."

"Nuts are more of a treasure than gold to squirrels," said the squirrel.

Stripey and Getup trotted off down the garden path.

"Look," Getup stopped and scraped at the path with her little woollen hoof. "A trapdoor!"

"It must lead to the mole's tunnel Gumpa and Woeful found once," cried Stripey. "Let's look for treasure in the tunnel!"

They lifted the trapdoor and peered into the darkness.

Leaving the trapdoor open for light, they trotted down the steps and along the tunnel. It wound and twisted and other shadowy tunnels joined it.

"I don't like it," whispered Stripey.

But when they turned to go back, they didn't know which tunnel was which. Somewhere deep down in the dark damp earth, they were lost!

Meanwhile Woeful had climbed on to the garage roof. His friend Jick the jackdaw stowed treasure under a broken tile.

"Found anything new recently?" asked Woeful.

"Caw!" said Jick, and pulled out a beautiful diamond ring.

"Lend it to me for our treasure hunt!" begged Woeful. "The others won't know that I didn't find it."

All this time poor Gumpa was still dangling. He couldn't get down and he grew more and more furious.

"Someone should come and look for me!" he fumed. "But nobody cares about me. I could dangle here for days and nobody would bother! Poor me."

High up in the tree sat Little Mut and the squirrel.

"How small the garden looks miles below," squeaked
Little Mut. "There's a bit of green stuff waving near the sundial!"

"It's just an old duster or something," said squirrel. "Here's
an acorn to take home."

As Little Mut reached the ground, he met Woeful.

"I've got a magnificent treasure!" boasted the little monkey, "but you can't see it until we all meet."

"Listen!" squeaked Little Mut. "What was that?"

Far away, they heard someone calling "Help! Help!"

"It's Stripey," cried Little Mut. "He's in trouble!"

"It comes from Splashing Stream!" gasped Woeful.

They hopped and jumped as fast as they could, out of the garden into the wood until they reached Splashing Stream.

Then they stopped and gasped . . .

There were Getup and Stripey in a cave on the other side of Splashing Stream and they had a mysterious padlocked box!

"We've found treasure! But we got lost in the tunnel and came out here," explained Getup.

"We'll get lost if we go back into the tunnel," called Stripey, "and we can't get out this way because of the water!"

"I know!" cried Woeful. "We'll go to the trapdoor and call down it, then you come towards our voices. We'll soon have you out!"

He and Little Mut raced for the trapdoor and knelt down on the path.

"Stripeee!" they yelled. "Getuuup!"

"This way! This way!" called Woeful.

Soon they heard the little Animals answering, "We're coming!" At last two shadowy forms carrying a shadowy something came trotting along the shadowy tunnel.

"Lend a paw!" cried Stripey. With much pulling and tugging, they heaved the mysterious box up on to the path.

"Hallo, Animals!" cried Timothy, coming out to play. "What have you got there?"

"**TREASURE**!" they told him.

"That's dad's cash box!" shouted Timothy. "It was stolen last year. The burglar must have dropped it as he ran away. You are clever Animals!"

Stripey and Getup beamed with pride.

Timothy rattled it. "Listen, it's still full of money!"

"I found treasure too," squeaked Little Mut, showing them the acorn.

"Wait till you see my treasure!" boasted Woeful, smiling from ear to ear. "It's far better than yours." He took off his hat and felt for the ring and . . . there was nothing there!

"It's gone!" he gasped. "It must have fallen out. It was a beautiful diamond ring!"

"Rubbish!" said the others. "You're always pretending, Woeful. Let's go and tell Timothy's dad we've found his cashbox!"

Woeful crept away. "They won't ever believe I found a diamond ring," he thought sadly. "I'll never be able to find it again. It might have dropped anywhere."

Little Mut brought Woeful a sandwich and tried to cheer him up.

"It was fun seeing the garden from the top of squirrel's tree," he told him. "I could even see an old green duster near the sundial." But Woeful didn't answer.

"Well, if you won't talk to me, I'll go back to the others," said Little Mut. "Do come in for tea, Woeful."

When Woeful joined the others, Gumpa was still missing. Gumpa and Woeful quarrel a lot but they are really best friends.

Gumpa was still missing at suppertime and Woeful was so miserable he couldn't eat.

By bedtime, the wind howled outside. "Gumpa will be so cold," he worried. "He only has his thin green coat on."

Suddenly Woeful sprang up. "Green coat! Little Mut said a green duster . . . near the sundial!"

Off he went, bounding downstairs and out of the house to the sundial and . . . there was Gumpa, still dangling! Woeful helped the poor cold bear down.

"Thank you, Woeful," said Gumpa. "You are a true friend to come and find me."

The little friends walked arm in arm down the path and Woeful told Gumpa about the ring he had found and lost.

"The others don't believe me," he said.

"I believe you," comforted Gumpa.

Suddenly Woeful stopped. There, on the path in the moonlight, twinkled the diamond ring!

They raced back to the house and showed it to Timothy.

"Why, it's mum's ring!" he squealed and woke the whole house up. Timothy's mum and dad promised them all a picnic at the seaside the next day.

Timothy lifted his Animals safely up on to their Shelf.

"I'm very proud of you all," he told them. "You are the most special Animals in the world!"